RUCK IN THE MUCK

Ruck in the Muck

Ceri Wyn Jones

Illustrated by
Adrian Reynolds

Pont

Beyond the old barbed wire
we found a field of play,
a field for games of rugby
behind our house all day.

The field is full of squelches,
of reeds and weeds and wet,
where thistles and sheep droppings
and cowpats are a threat.

Without its oil and engine
an old Land Rover sits,
just like the rusty tractor,
all stones and bones and bits.

But, like my big, big brother,
I know this field of fame
is our Millennium Stadium
once we begin our game.

The sheep are our supporters,
the crows are on their feet;
the blackbird brings his whistle
to ref the game, 'Tweet, tweet!'

My brother's always England,
and I am always Wales,
and though we're real buddies,
we battle hard as nails.

The fans are all bleating,
the stadium is tense:
we start when my brother
kicks off from the fence.

The oval ball rises
as high as the tree,
then falls like an acorn
at speed towards me.

My head's spinning skywards,
the reeds grab my toes,
before the ball bounces
and bombs on my nose.

I want to start crying
and run home to Mum,
but, no, I am braver
so Fee, Fie, Fo, Fum . . .

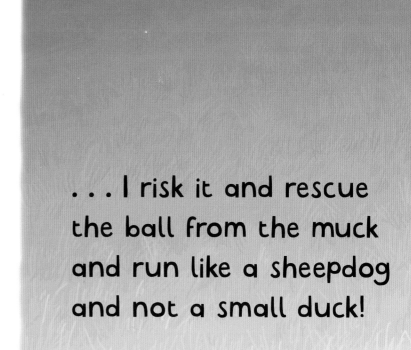

. . . I risk it and rescue
the ball from the muck
and run like a sheepdog
and not a small duck!

I scurry, I squirrel,
I leap like a lamb;
I gallop and go like
the sprinter I am.

I jink past the tractor
and dummy the weeds,
and gracefully glide past
the thistles and reeds.

But my brother Samson's
as hard as a post:
he tackles and folds me
in half, like some toast.

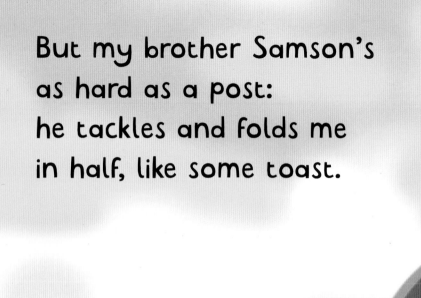

Next, Samson's decided
that *he* wants a scrum
to push, twist and crush me
as small as a crumb.

The Englishman grabs me
but from him I fly:
yes, Wales really needs me,
I must score a try.

The try line is calling,
the wind's in my hair,
my heart's beating faster
and I'm almost there.

The only two things that
can now stop me dead
are Samson behind me
and cowpats ahead!

As Samson gets nearer
through squelches and slime,
I suddenly sidestep
the cowpats in time.

But Samson the Tackler,
he dives for my toes . . .
Too late! In a cowpat
he lands on his nose!

I've now crossed the try line
(the edge of the hedge)
and scored in the corner —
I must be a Ledge!

Just one last conversion
on this field of dreams
will settle the battle
between the two teams.

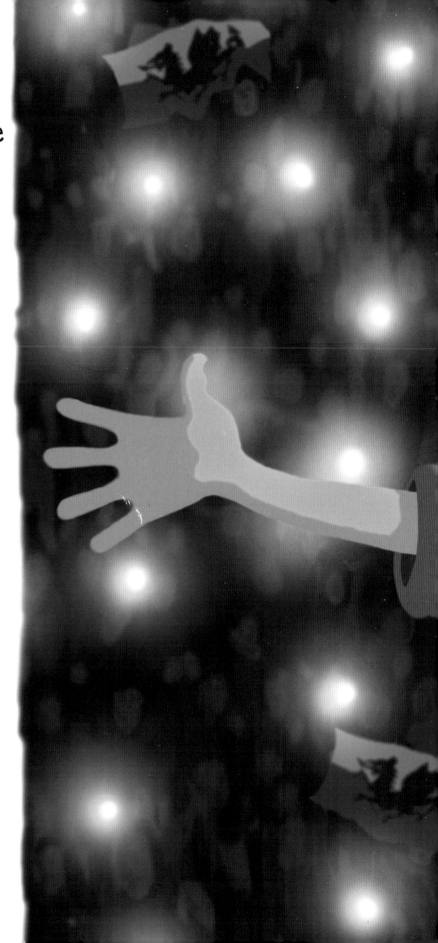

The ball is placed neatly
on top of the tee
(a medium-sized molehill):
it's now up to me.

Above the Land Rover,
between posts, it flies
and over the crossbar –
and Samson just cries.

Then Mum shouts out, 'It's teatime!'
which means it's going-hometime:
far more important than the tries
is custard-pies-and-caketime.

In spite of that conversion,
we leave the field in union:

it's teatime now for me, I know;
it's bathtime, though, for Samson!

First published in 2015 by Pont Books, an imprint of
Gomer Press, Llandysul, Ceredigion, SA44 4JL
www.gomer.co.uk

ISBN 978 1 78562 067 6

A CIP record for this title is available from the British Library.

This book is published with the financial support of the Welsh Books Council.

Printed and bound in Wales at Gomer Press, Llandysul, Ceredigion